DR. & MR. JEKYLL HYDE

Adapted and Illustrated by
Jason Ho

Based upon the works of
Robert Louis Stevenson

magic
wagon

visit us at
www.abdopublishing.com

Published by Magic Wagon, a division of the ABDO Publishing Group, 8000 West 78th Street, Edina, Minnesota 55439. Copyright © 2008 by Abdo Consulting Group, Inc. International copyrights reserved in all countries. All rights reserved. No part of this book may be reproduced in any form without written permission from the publisher. Graphic Planet™ is a trademark and logo of Magic Wagon.

Printed in the United States.

Based upon the works of Robert Louis Stevenson
Written & Illustrated by Jason Ho
Colored & Lettered by Jay Fotos
Edited & Directed by Chazz DeMoss
Cover Design by Neil Klinepier

Library of Congress Cataloging-in-Publication Data

Ho, Jason.
  Dr. Jekyll & Mr. Hyde / written and illustrated by Jason Ho ; based upon the works of Robert Louis Stevenson.
     p. cm. -- (Graphic horror)
  ISBN 978-1-60270-058-1
  1. Graphic novels. I. Stevenson, Robert Louis, 1850-1894. Dr. Jekyll & Mr. Hyde. II. Title.
  PN6727.H56D7 2008
  741.5'973--dc22
                                                    2007009616

Mr. Enfield was a well-established man of the city. And Mr. Utterson was a known lawyer. They both looked forward to their Sunday excursions. On this particular day, they happened upon a bystreet in the heart of London.

A few doors from a corner stood a sinister looking building.

Pointing with his cane, Mr. Enfield remarked, "Have you ever noticed this door?" When Mr. Utterson acknowledged that he had, Enfield added, "I've been here before, under strange circumstances."

"On my way home from some other matter, it was about three o'clock on a black morning. I spied a little man strutting along, and a girl about eight or ten running hard from a cross street. Naturally, they collided. But the fiendish thing is, the man calmly trampled over the child, leaving her screaming on the ground.

"I hollered, chased him down and collared him. He did not resist, but gave a glare so ugly it brought out a sweat from within me.

"The child was looked after by the doctor, whom she was originally sent for. While I attempted to keep the mother off him as best I could.

"It was agreed that the matter would be put to rest with payment. At that point we were led to that very door. He came foward with ten pounds in gold and a check."

"I was sure that the check was a forgery, but was assured that every bit of it was genuine.

"Then Mr. Utterson asked, "I'd like to know the name of the man who walked over the girl." "It was a man by the name of Hyde," said Mr. Enfield. "What did he look like?" asked Mr. Utterson.

"He is not easy to describe, there was something disagreeable and detestable about him. I never met a man I so disliked, yet I'm unsure as to why.

"That very night, Utterson went into his business room and got a document from his safe. It was endorsed as Dr. Jekyll's will. It said that upon Henry Jekyll's death or disappearance, his possessions are to be passed into the hands of Edward Hyde.

"This effected Utterson greatly, and he sought help from an old friend, Dr. Lanyon. Dr. Lanyon, Dr. Jekyll and Mr. Utterson were very old and close friends, though he has seen little of Henry Jekyll lately. And when asked about Edward Hyde, Lanyon replied:

"Hyde? No, I've never heard of him."

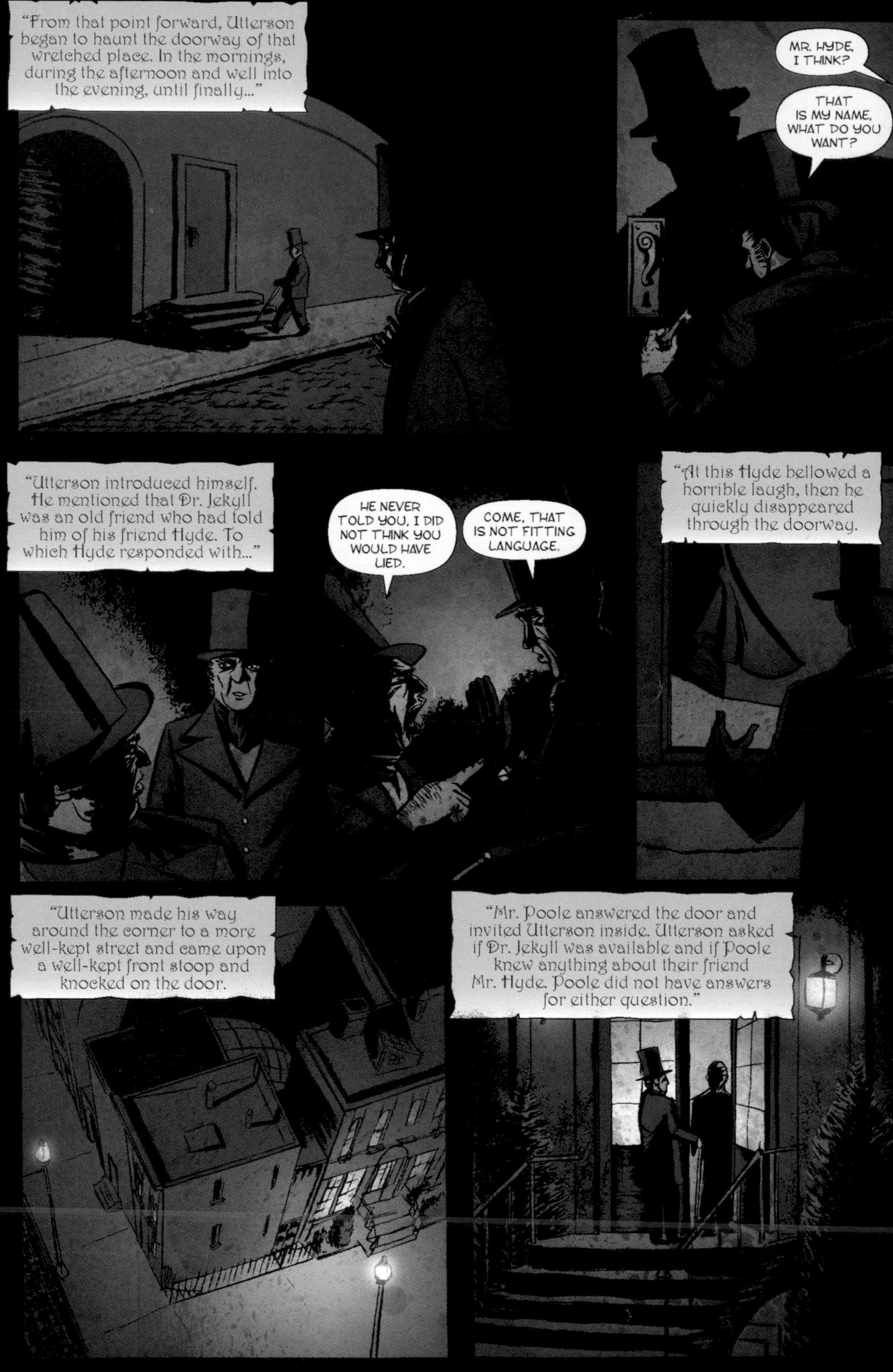
"From that point forward, Utterson began to haunt the doorway of that wretched place. In the mornings, during the afternoon and well into the evening, until finally..."
MR. HYDE, I THINK?
THAT IS MY NAME, WHAT DO YOU WANT?
"Utterson introduced himself. He mentioned that Dr. Jekyll was an old friend who had told him of his friend Hyde. To which Hyde responded with..."
HE NEVER TOLD YOU, I DID NOT THINK YOU WOULD HAVE LIED.
COME, THAT IS NOT FITTING LANGUAGE.
"At this Hyde bellowed a horrible laugh, then he quickly disappeared through the doorway.
"Utterson made his way around the corner to a more well-kept street and came upon a well-kept front stoop and knocked on the door.
"Mr. Poole answered the door and invited Utterson inside. Utterson asked if Dr. Jekyll was available and if Poole knew anything about their friend Mr. Hyde. Poole did not have answers for either question."

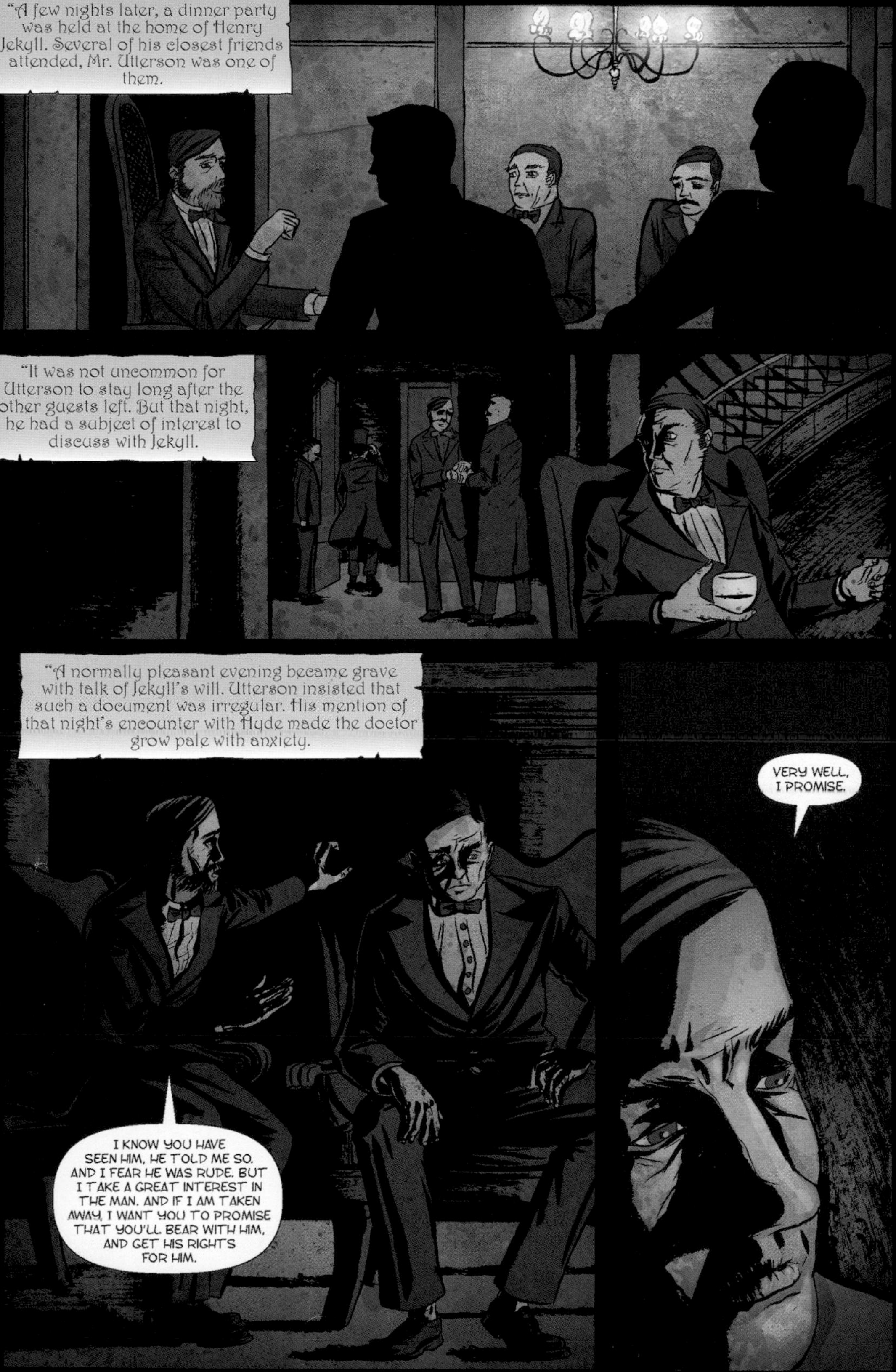
"A few nights later, a dinner party was held at the home of Henry Jekyll. Several of his closest friends attended, Mr. Utterson was one of them.
"It was not uncommon for Utterson to stay long after the other guests left. But that night, he had a subject of interest to discuss with Jekyll.
"A normally pleasant evening became grave with talk of Jekyll's will. Utterson insisted that such a document was irregular. His mention of that night's encounter with Hyde made the doctor grow pale with anxiety.
I KNOW YOU HAVE SEEN HIM, HE TOLD ME SO. AND I FEAR HE WAS RUDE. BUT I TAKE A GREAT INTEREST IN THE MAN. AND IF I AM TAKEN AWAY, I WANT YOU TO PROMISE THAT YOU'LL BEAR WITH HIM, AND GET HIS RIGHTS FOR HIM.
VERY WELL, I PROMISE.

"Nearly a year later, an unspeakable crime occurred, and was made more notable by the high position of the victim. A young woman who had been at the window saw a man approach another on the street. The pleasant looking individual began speaking to the other, who without cause began to beat him.

"Upon inspection there was nothing to be found with the victim except half a piece of a broken cane and a letter addressed to Mr. Utterson.

"The next morning, the police brought the letter and part of a walking cane to Mr. Utterson. Utterson immediately recognized the half of cane as one he had given as a gift to Dr. Jekyll.

"Both the inspector and Mr. Utterson set forth to the doorway of Mr. Edward Hyde. Upon being let in, they found the place ransacked. To the delight of the inspector the other half of the cane was discovered."

"The next afternoon Utterson was admitted by Poole into Jekyll's private room.

"There, Utterson found Dr. Jekyll in a most distraught state. It was at this point that Jekyll produced a letter in Hyde's own hand. It stated Hyde's intention to escape. It was a relief to Utterson to know that Jekyll would have no more to do with that man.

"Later that evening, Utterson sat down in a state of exhaustion. With him was his head clerk Mr. Guest, who was aware of the current situation. Guest was also a student and critic of handwriting. It was this expertise that Utterson sought.

"Just then, the maid entered with a dinner invitation from Dr. Jekyll. Mr. Guest then compared Jekyll's note to that of Hyde's.

"Mr. Guest found a curious thing about both notes. They were written by the same person."

"Time went on and the search for Hyde had quieted down. During this time, Jekyll had once again begun to show himself to the world. He began to have guests and be lively once again.

"One evening, Utterson and Lanyon were invited to dinner at Dr. Jekyll's home. The three were inseparable as if nothing terrible had ever happened.

"What he found was disturbing to say the least. Lanyon was in a dire state. He had withered away into something less than he used to be."

I HAVE HAD A SHOCK, FROM WHICH I SHALL NEVER RECOVER FROM.

JEKYLL IS ILL TOO, HAVE YOU BEEN ABLE TO SEE HIM?

I DON'T WANT TO SEE OR HEAR OF HIM AGAIN.

I AM QUITE DONE WITH HIM, SO PLEASE DON'T EVER SPEAK OF HIM AGAIN.

"The next day, Utterson was denied entrance to Jekyll's home. On the fourth it was the same. Utterson finally decided to visit Dr. Lanyon.

"A week afterward, Lanyon was dead. Utterson received a letter from Lanyon. It had the incitation: "Private, for the hand of G.J. Utterson alone, in the case of his death, to be destroyed unread."

"Though curious of what it could contain, Utterson respected the wishes of his friend. He placed it in his safe unopened.

"At that point, Utterson attempted to once again see Jekyll. He was stopped by Poole.

"It was another Sunday that Mr. Enfield and Mr. Utterson found their way through that part of town which brought them to the doorway."

"Utterson opened the envelope only to find another sealed envelope. On it was written: "Not to be opened until the death or disappearance of Dr. Henry Jekyll."

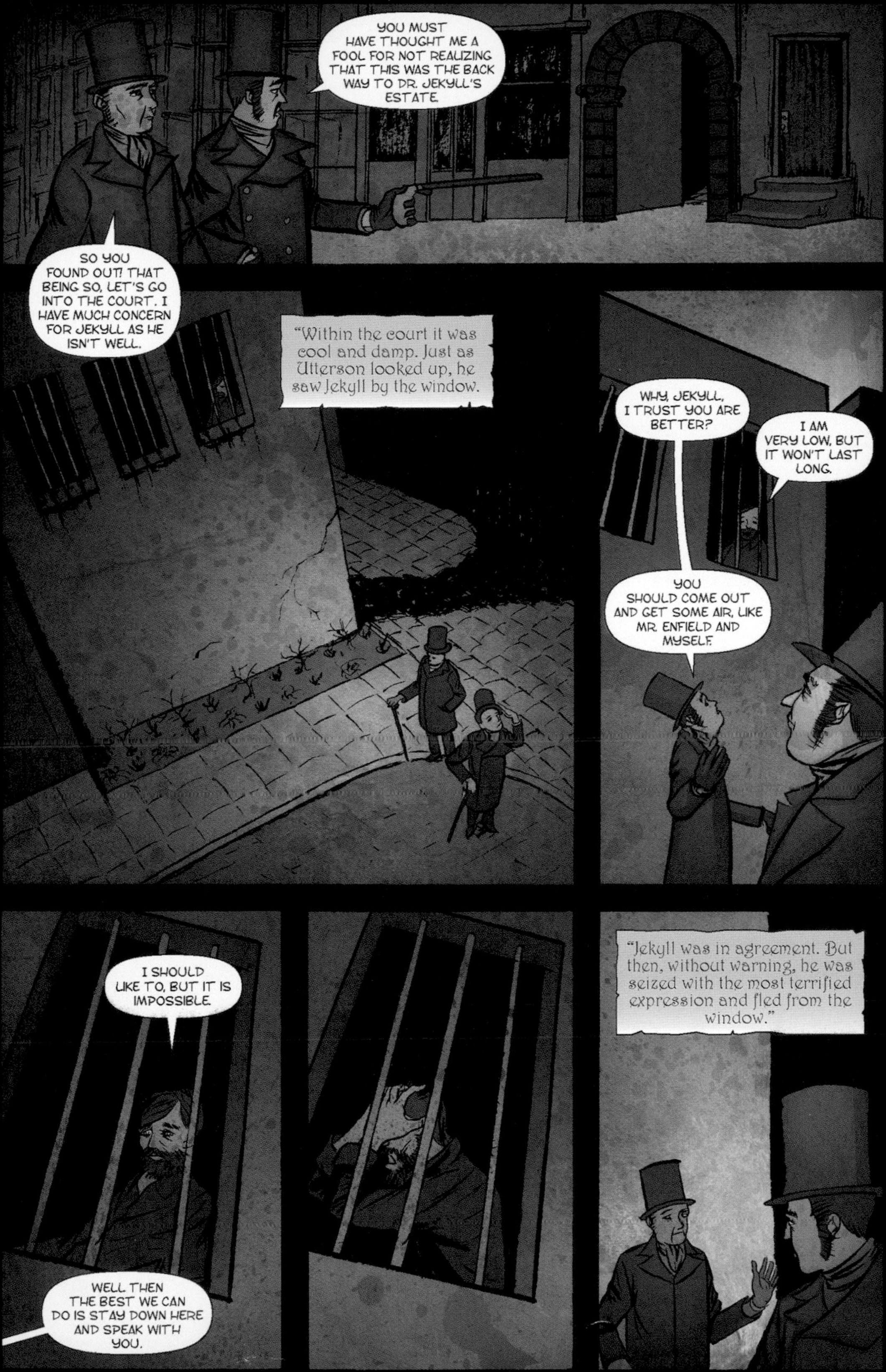

YOU MUST HAVE THOUGHT ME A FOOL FOR NOT REALIZING THAT THIS WAS THE BACK WAY TO DR. JEKYLL'S ESTATE.
SO YOU FOUND OUT! THAT BEING SO, LET'S GO INTO THE COURT. I HAVE MUCH CONCERN FOR JEKYLL AS HE ISN'T WELL.
"Within the court it was cool and damp. Just as Utterson looked up, he saw Jekyll by the window.
WHY, JEKYLL, I TRUST YOU ARE BETTER?
I AM VERY LOW, BUT IT WON'T LAST LONG.
YOU SHOULD COME OUT AND GET SOME AIR, LIKE MR. ENFIELD AND MYSELF.
I SHOULD LIKE TO, BUT IT IS IMPOSSIBLE.
WELL THEN THE BEST WE CAN DO IS STAY DOWN HERE AND SPEAK WITH YOU.
"Jekyll was in agreement. But then, without warning, he was seized with the most terrified expression and fled from the window."

"Mr. Utterson was relaxing after dinner, when Poole entered with a worrisome look upon his face."

I HAVE BEEN CONCERNED FOR A WEEK AS TO THE STATE OF DR. JEKYLL, BUT NOW SOMETHING IS VERY WRONG. YOU MUST COME AND SEE FOR YOURSELF.

"Utterson grabbed his coat and left with Poole into the night. When they entered the home of Dr. Jekyll, Utterson found the all the servants together and most afraid."

AND NOW, MR. UTTERSON, WALK WITH ME AS QUIETLY AS YOU CAN.

"They made their way through the courtyard and into the surgical theatre and then to the steps of Jekyll's private room."

SIR, MR. UTTERSON IS HERE TO SEE YOU.

TELL HIM I CANNOT SEE ANYONE.

"Poole was in Dr. Jeykll's employ for well over twenty years, he was sure he knew his own masters voice. And that voice from within was not it."

THAT VOICE FROM INSIDE HAS BEEN CRYING FOR SOME SORT OF MEDICINE ALL WEEK.

I HAD BEEN GIVEN LISTS TO BE SENT TO ALL THE CHEMISTS IN TOWN, BUT EVERY TIME, I AM TOLD TO FIND ANOTHER SOURCE, FOR WHATEVER I BRING IS IMPURE OR OF BAD QUALITY.

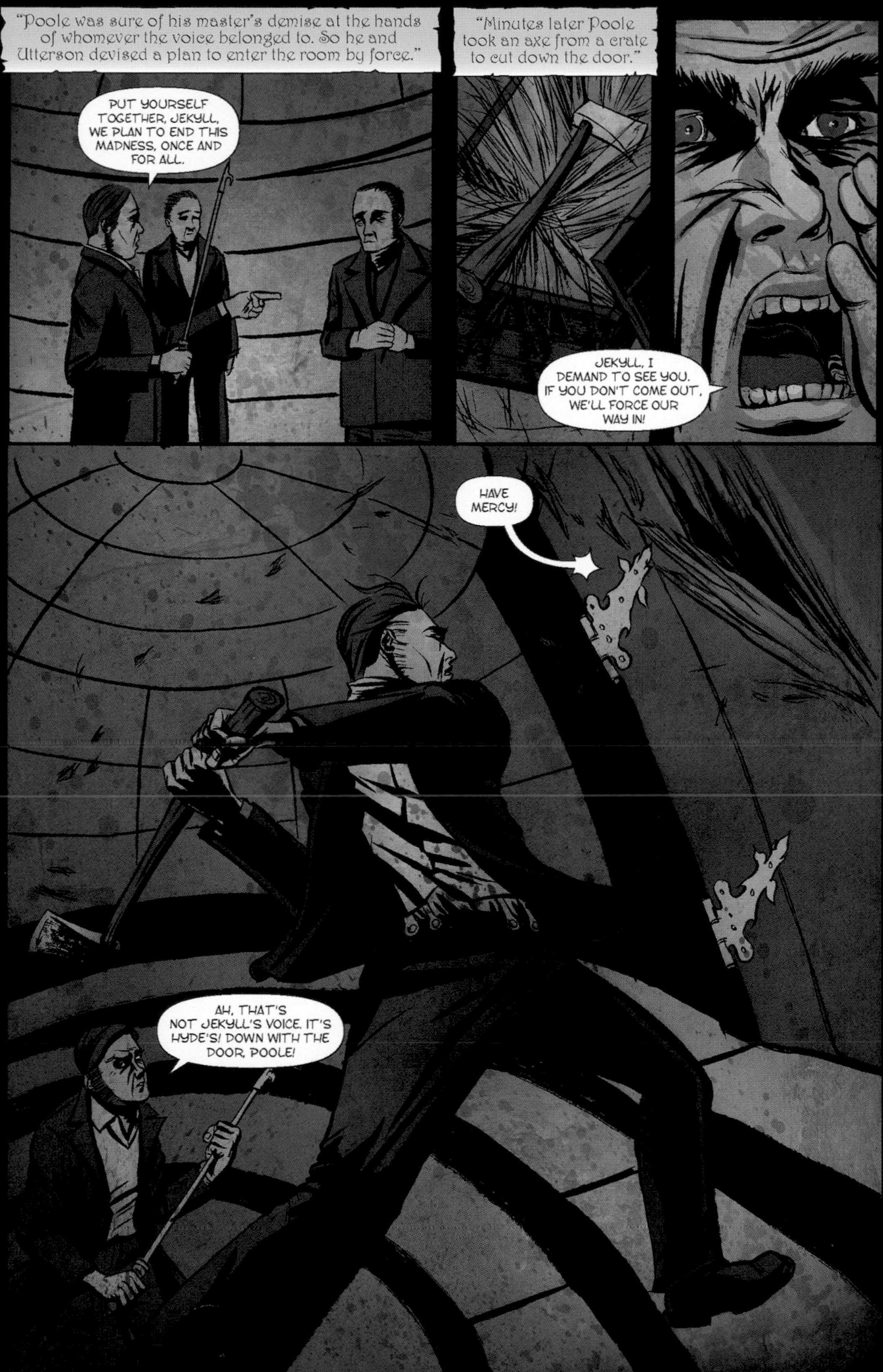
"Poole was sure of his master's demise at the hands of whomever the voice belonged to. So he and Utterson devised a plan to enter the room by force."
PUT YOURSELF TOGETHER, JEKYLL, WE PLAN TO END THIS MADNESS, ONCE AND FOR ALL.
"Minutes later Poole took an axe from a crate to cut down the door."
JEKYLL, I DEMAND TO SEE YOU. IF YOU DON'T COME OUT, WE'LL FORCE OUR WAY IN!
HAVE MERCY!
AH, THAT'S NOT JEKYLL'S VOICE. IT'S HYDE'S! DOWN WITH THE DOOR, POOLE!

"Poole rained down a series of blows upon the door until finally, it gave in.

"There on the floor lay a body still twitching. It was not Dr. Jekyll, but Edward Hyde. Next to him lay a crushed glass which had contatined some sort of vile liquid.

"They searched everywhere for Jekyll.

"But he was nowhere to be found.

"It was thought that he might have fled.

"But the rusted key that opened the rear entrance had been smashed.

"Later they re-entered the private room. There they discovered some documents which were dated that day. Also found were letters, letters addressed to Utterson."

DON'T SAY ANYTHING OF THIS. IF DR. JEKYLL HAS FLED OR IS DEAD, THE LEAST WE CAN DO IS SAVE HIS CREDIT.

I'M HEADED HOME TO STUDY THE INFORMATION GATHERED HERE TONIGHT. LATER I WILL RETURN AND WE WILL CALL THE POLICE.

"Four days ago, I received a letter from Henry Jekyll. It was strange not only because we are not in the habit of sending each other messages, but also of what was written."

"I was to head to his home and retrieve some items that were in his private study. In order to do so, I requested the help of a locksmith and a carpenter."

"Both arrived just after I did.

"They immediately set upon the door lock.

"Finally both the door and cabinet were breached. I took the requested items and left.

"Inspecting the contents of the box, I found a wrapper of some salt-like substance. Along with a bottle of red liquid, the smell of which was quite strong...

"There was also a journal with entries dating back several years. Peppered here and there were additions to some of the entries, saying "Double" and in some instances, "Total failure."

"All of this made me curious as to what it could mean. I would have to wait a few more hours to find that out."

"I had no understanding of what or why these items were so important. But to be cautious, I loaded a revolver for a sense of assurance.

"Midnight had rung, when there was a faint knock at the door."

ARE YOU THE FRIEND OF DR. JEKYLL'S?

YES.

"I invited him in. Before doing so he looked back as if sure he was being followed. This made me anxious and I thought about the revolver in my pocket.

"After a few steps inside my home, a fire was lit within his eyes as he said:"

DO YOU HAVE IT? DID YOU BRING IT HERE?

COME SIR, I DON'T EVEN KNOW WHO YOU ARE. PLEASE WON'T YOU TAKE A SEAT?

I APOLOGIZE. PLEASE FORGIVE MY RUDENESS.

"But I could see that he was anxious and that impatience was ready to burst forth.

WELL, THERE IT IS, SIR.

"The little man took the ingredients with haste and set about mixing a portion of each chemical into a glass.

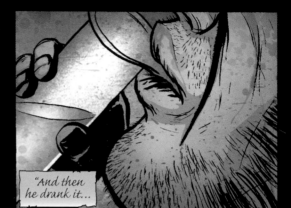

"And then he drank it...

"At once he staggered and began to shake and scream in agony, gasping for breath."

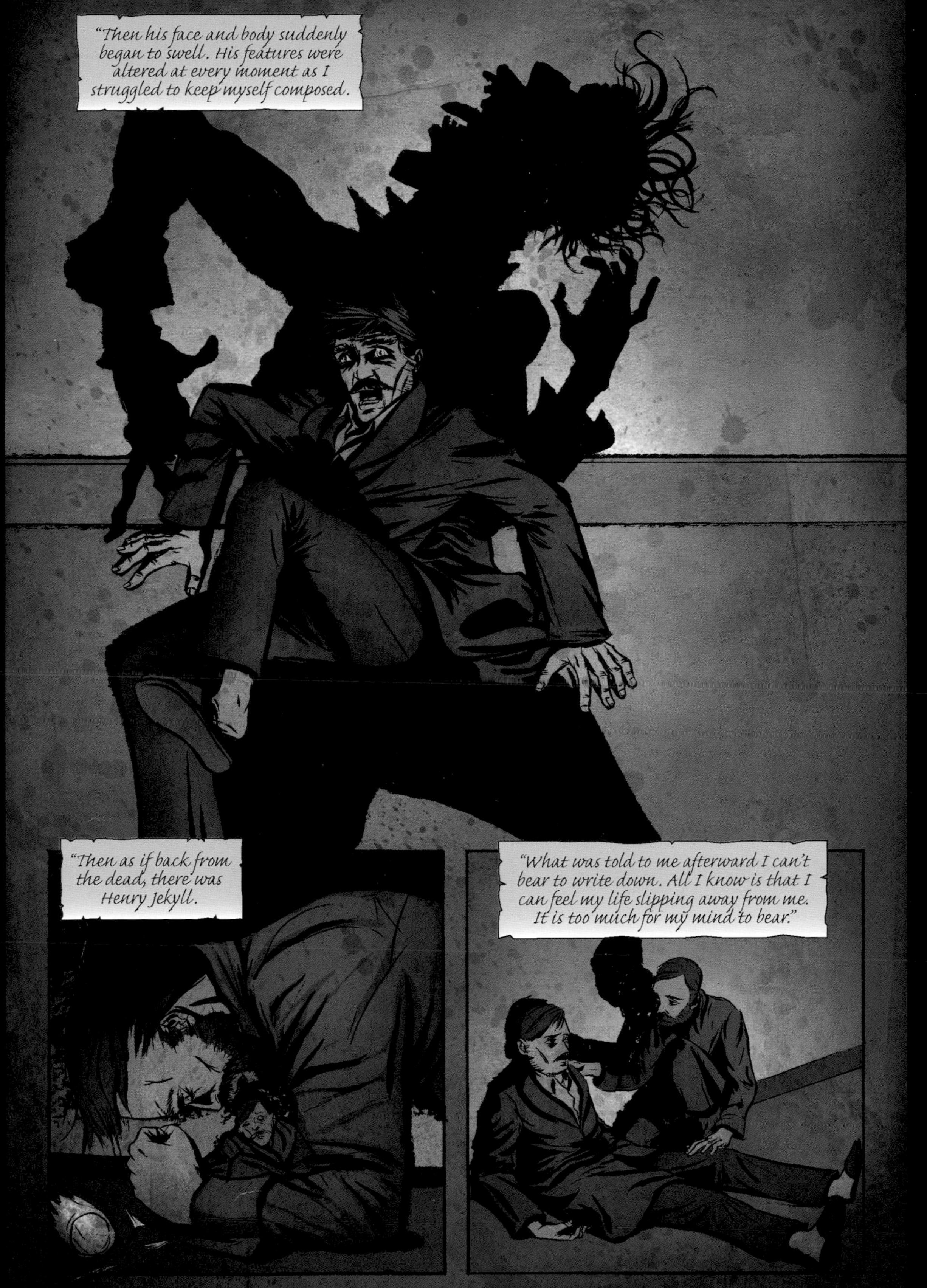
"Then his face and body suddenly began to swell. His features were altered at every moment as I struggled to keep myself composed.
"Then as if back from the dead, there was Henry Jekyll.
"What was told to me afterward I can't bear to write down. All I know is that I can feel my life slipping away from me. It is too much for my mind to bear."

"I know now that what I had done was horrible. But my interest in separating the good from the evil was too great.

"It was my sincere desire to be able to split the man that was evil from the man that was good. So that they could lead two different lives without influencing the other.

"When I had reached the point where it was time to test the theory, I took it upon myself to do such a thing."

"I had felt my self changed. At once I was new and free. So free that I felt as though I could do anything I pleased.

"There were no mirrors in my private laboratory, so I snuck into the house like a thief. I went into my own bedroom to get a look at what I had become.

"Instead of being horrified, I was pleased at what I had become. I welcomed the change, and at the same time I felt as though I was myself.

"It was only later that I realized that more and more Edward Hyde was slowly taking over, and the evil brewing within him wanted to come out."

"It was when I was constantly fighting the urge to let Hyde loose that I was part of a crime. It was not so terrible, as it was cruel.

"Two months before the murder of that poor man, I had come home from a night of adventure as Mr. Hyde. But I found myself not in Hyde's room, but in my own bedroom.

"I couldn't understand how it had happened, I had to get to the laboratory before anyone saw me like that.

"I dressed as well as I could and headed towards the laboratory. Unfortunately, Poole saw me running about before I could make it outside.

"However I made it to my private room safely. I mixed some of the drink, which changed me into my normal self."

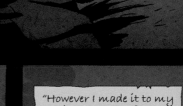

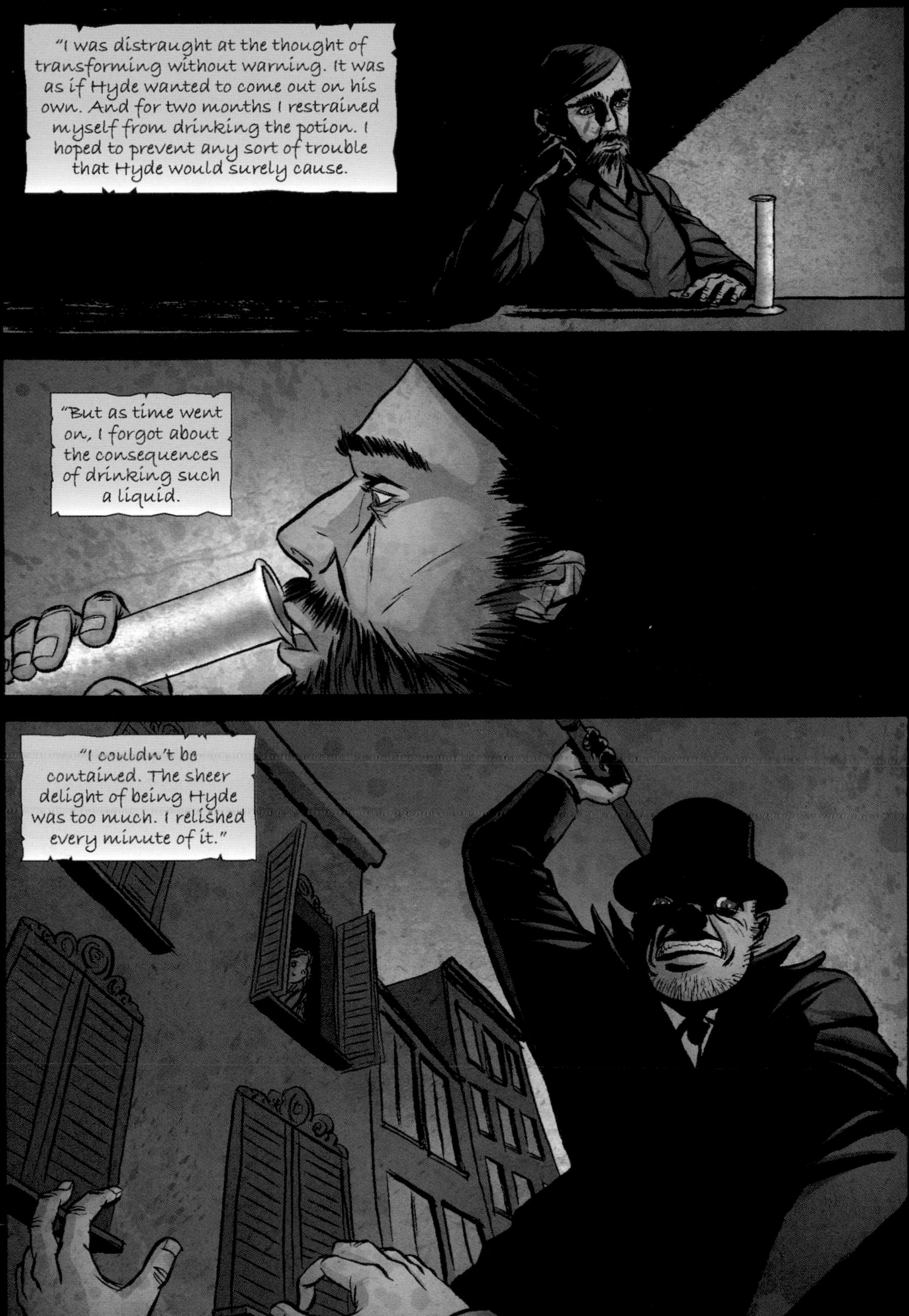
"I was distraught at the thought of transforming without warning. It was as if Hyde wanted to come out on his own. And for two months I restrained myself from drinking the potion. I hoped to prevent any sort of trouble that Hyde would surely cause.
"But as time went on, I forgot about the consequences of drinking such a liquid.
"I couldn't be contained. The sheer delight of being Hyde was too much. I relished every minute of it."

"I came back to myself after drinking the potion. I was thankful that it was over. The guilt within me was strong and I promised myself never again would I drink the mixture.

"Looking back, I remember how devious Hyde had become. After committing an act of murder, he began burning any and all papers that would connect him and his terrible crime.

"At that point, I made a decision to step back into the world of man and join my friends as Dr. Henry Jekyll."

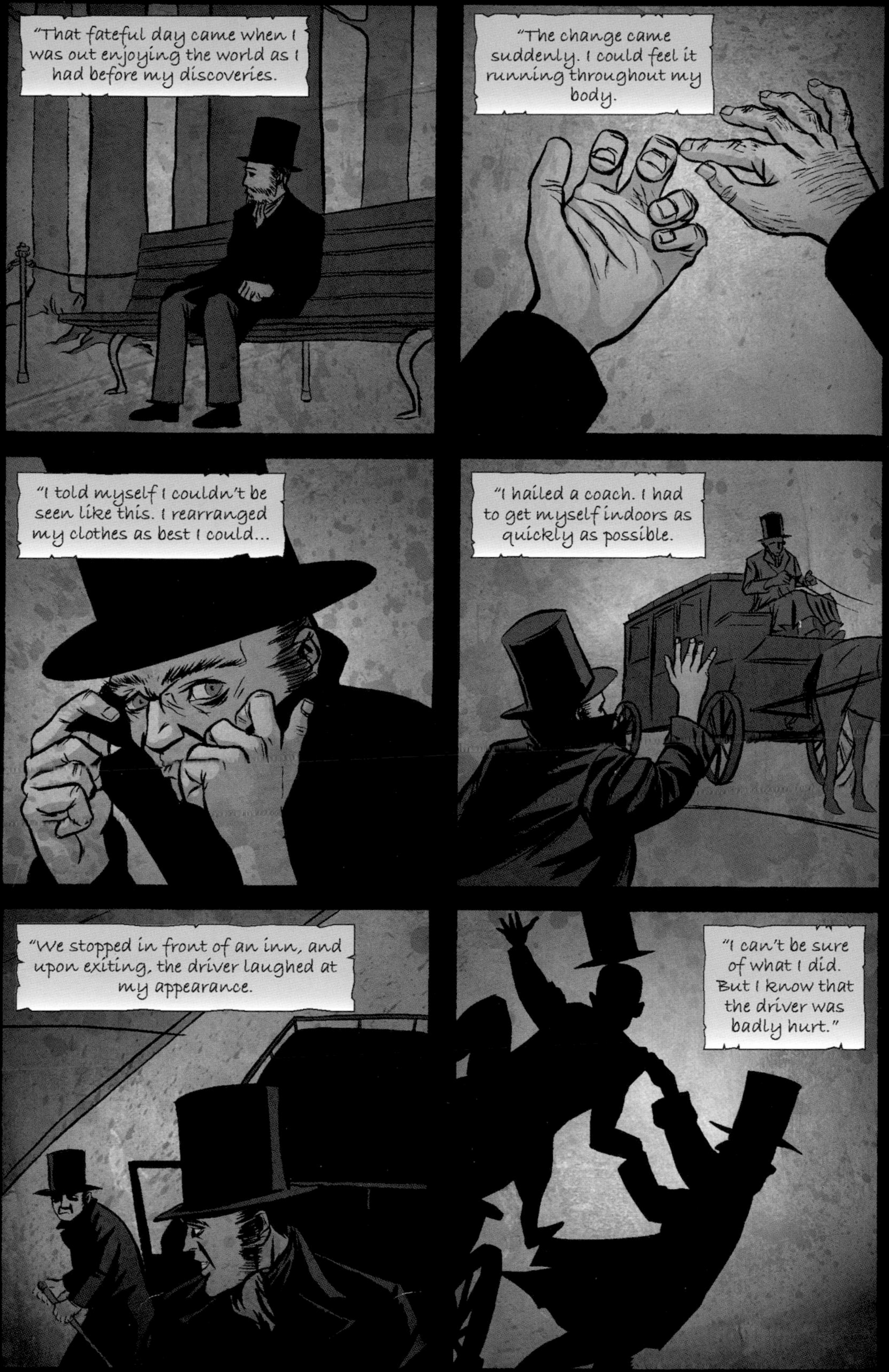
"That fateful day came when I was out enjoying the world as I had before my discoveries.
"The change came suddenly. I could feel it running throughout my body.
"I told myself I couldn't be seen like this. I rearranged my clothes as best I could...
"I hailed a coach. I had to get myself indoors as quickly as possible.
"We stopped in front of an inn, and upon exiting, the driver laughed at my appearance.
"I can't be sure of what I did. But I know that the driver was badly hurt."

"At the inn, I showed such an ugly face that it scared the servants.

"The attendant that took the letters to be sent off to Dr. Lanyon and Poole was also afraid to look at me.

"After that, I sat in the room waiting for time to go by. Eventually, I took another coach in order to get to Dr. Lanyon's home."

"Exiting the coach, I was approached by a woman selling lights.

"The anger inside of Hyde came out in one swift blow.

"When I came too at Lanyon's, I was concerned at the state that Lanyon had been reduced to.

"Lanyon was disgusted and appalled at the sight of me...

"He began to scream. What he said I don't really know, but I left tired and not my regular self."

"I went home to bed and immediately fell asleep. But I was haunted by nightmares that I could not wake from.

"I woke up refreshed, hoping that this was the end. But it wasn't to last. I felt the pangs of transformation coming too.

"I ran back to my laboratory so I could stop Hyde from coming back. And it lasted for some time..."

"It lasted for a short time, but I could feel Hyde trying to escape. The thought of this made me both physically and mentally tired.

"Eventually it wore off and Hyde reappeared.

"A week had passed and I was down to a small amount of salts needed to stop the change. Poole was sent to fetch me more of the salts...

"But none of the new supply would work.

"I believe that the supply I had orginally bought was somehow not pure. It is this difference that had turned me into what I am now. I don't know what it is or how much of a difference it is that makes me change."

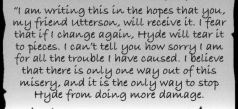

"I am writing this in the hopes that you, my friend Utterson, will receive it. I fear that if I change again, Hyde will tear it to pieces. I can't tell you how sorry I am for all the trouble I have caused. I believe that there is only one way out of this misery, and it is the only way to stop Hyde from doing more damage.

I will seal this letter, addressed to you, as my full confession. And may you please forgive me.

Your sad friend, Dr. Henry Jekyll.

JEKYLL, I **DEMAND** TO SEE YOU!

Robert Louis Stevenson

Robert Louis Stevenson was born on November 13, 1850, in Edinburgh, Scotland. He was the only son of Thomas Stevenson and Margaret Isabella Balfour. Robert was often sick as a child and did not attend school regularly.

At age 17, Stevenson entered the Edinburgh University, where he was supposed to study engineering. Instead, he began to study law. In 1875, Stevenson was called to the Scottish bar, but never practiced.

Stevenson traveled often and his travels provided much to write about. Slowly, his writing career developed. His travel stories first appeared in magazines and later in novels. They grew in popularity and he later became well-known.

In 1880, Stevenson married American Fanny Vandegrift Osbourne. He continued to travel with his wife and stepson, Lloyd Osbourne. He visited America, the South Seas, and Samoa.

The Stevensons settled in Samoa in 1890. The climate there was good for Stevenson's health. He was very active until he died suddenly on December 3, 1894. Today, Robert Louis Stevenson is best known for his novels of adventure and suspense.

Stevenson has many Additional Works including

Treasure Island (1883)

A Child's Garden of Verses (1885)

Strange Case of Dr. Jekyll and Mr. Hyde (1886)

Kidnapped (1886)

The Master of Ballantrae (1889)

Kidnapped: The Ebb-Tide (1894)

Glossary

demise - the end of an activity or life.

distraught - upset with doubt or painful thoughts.

endorse - to sign your name to something.

excursions - a trip or expedition.

forgery - falsely making or altering a document, such as a check.

inscription - the wording on a coin, medal, seal, or document.

sinister - a person or thing who looks dangerous or evil.

Web Sites

To learn more about Robert Louis Stevenson, visit ABDO
Publishing Company on the World Wide Web at
www.abdopublishing.com. Web sites about Stevenson are featured
on our Book Links page. These links are routinely monitored and
updated to provide the most current information available.